THE
DINOSAUR PRINCESS
and Other
Prehistoric Riddles

David A. Adler

illustrated by
Loreen Leedy

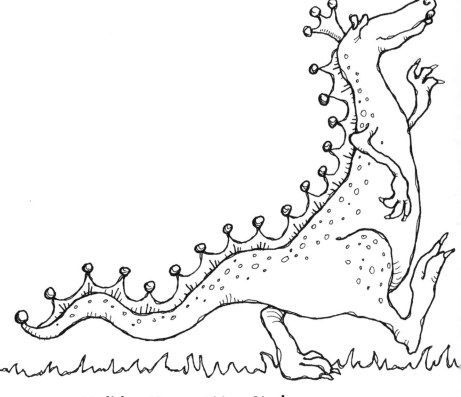

Holiday House / New York

To Eddie, who loves dinosaurs

Library of Congress Cataloging-in-Publication Data

Adler, David A.
The dinosaur princess and other prehistoric riddles.

Summary: A collection of jokes and riddles about
dinosaurs and cavemen, including "Why doesn't
anyone play with Brontous? He was a saur loser."
1. Riddles, Juvenile. 2. Dinosaurs—Juvenile
humor. [1. Dinosaurs—Wit and humor. 2. Jokes.
3. Riddles] I. Leedy, Loreen, ill. II. Title.
PN6371.5.A3224 1988   398'.6   87-25121
ISBN 0-8234-0686-5

THE
DINOSAUR PRINCESS
and Other
Prehistoric Riddles

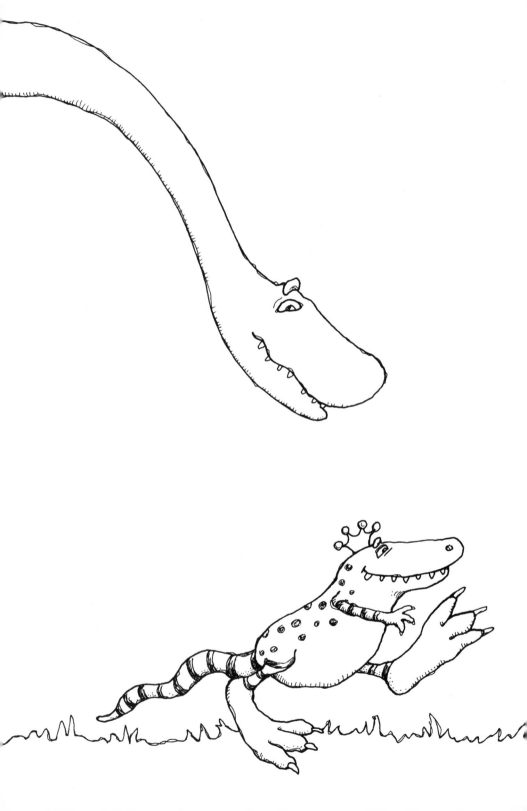

What's a caveman who has never been
to the big city?

A pre-hick-storic.

Why did Apatosaurus miss the train?

He got stuck in a turnstile.

What's the difference between cavemen and sewn socks?

Cavemen are dead men. Sewn socks are men-dead.

What's the name of the leaky dinosaur?

Bronto-porous.

How did scientists find the dinosaur princess?

They followed the dinosaur prints (prince).

What happened when Brachiosaurus walked
through the spinach fields?

He made creamed spinach.

Did woolly mammoths get ticks and fleas?

No, just moths.

What's a dinosaur curse?

A Tyrannosaurus hex.

How did cavemen and women make wooden tools?

A whittle at a time.

Did Tyrannosaurus Rex entertain a lot?

Sure. He always had friends for lunch.

The woolly mammoth is the ancestor of what animal?

The polyester mammoth.

How would you get milk and eggs from a dinosaur?

By stealing its shopping cart.

What kept cavemen and women up at night?

Dino-snores.

What would you get if you crossed a dinosaur with a game-show host?

A dead giveaway.

What did the cranky dinosaur tell the paleontologist?

"Don't jostle my fossil."

Why did dinosaurs turn into fossils?

When the band started to play, the music
made the dinosaurs rock.

What would you get if you crossed a cat
with Tyrannosaurus Rex?

A big ugly puss.

Where do dinosaurs still follow cavemen?

In the dictionary.

What do you get when you cross a dinosaur
with a magician?

A dino-sorcerer.

What steps did cavemen and women take to
protect themselves from dinosaurs?

Big steps.

Was it surprising when scientists first found dinosaur bones?

No. It was surprising they could lose anything that big.

What happened when Pteranodon flew into
a soda can?

Nothing. It was a soft drink.

How would you make stegosaurus soup?

In a big pot.

What did dinosaurs have that no other animals had?

Baby dinosaurs.

What happens when Apatosaurus beats the drums
and Allosaurus strums a guitar?

Tyrannosaurus rocks.

What does Triceratops sit on?

His tricera-bottom.

What's really old, has two tongues and lots of eyes?

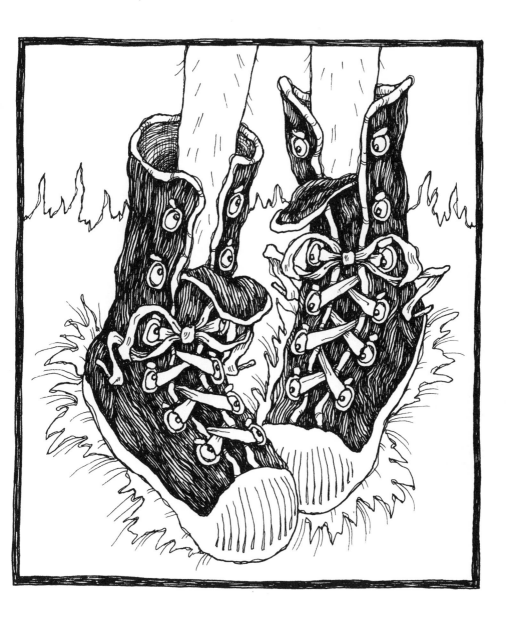

A cave woman's sneakers.

What would you get if you crossed Triceratops with a kangaroo?

Tricera-hops.

What would you say if you saw a three-headed dinosaur?

"Hello, hello, hello."

Name five members of the dinosaur family.

Mommy dinosaur, Daddy dinosaur and the
three baby dinosaurs.

What do you get when you cross a dinosaur with the back half of a horse?

A dead end.

What's inside every dinosaur?

A dino-core.

When did cavemen and women keep saying "please"
and "thank you"?

In the Nice Age.

Why didn't anyone play with Brontous?

He was a saur loser.

Where did Bagaceratops sleep?

In the riverbed.

How did Allosaurus get so rich?

He charged everyone he saw.

How would you make a dinosaur lighter?

Put some kerosene in his mouth and then
stick in a wick.

What followed the Mesozoic Age?

The Clean-up-zoic Age.

Why don't dinosaur skeletons get up and leave the museum?

They don't have the guts.

How would you spell ankylosaurus?

Slowly.

What would you give a seasick hadrosaurus?

Plenty of room.

Which prehistoric animal lived in a change purse?

The dimetrodon.

Was anyone safe from man-eating dinosaurs?

Sure, women and children.

What does Grandma Protoceratops carry in her wallet?

Photoceratops.

How do you get into a dinosaur cave?

By using a skeleton key.

What would you find in a dinosaur's ear?

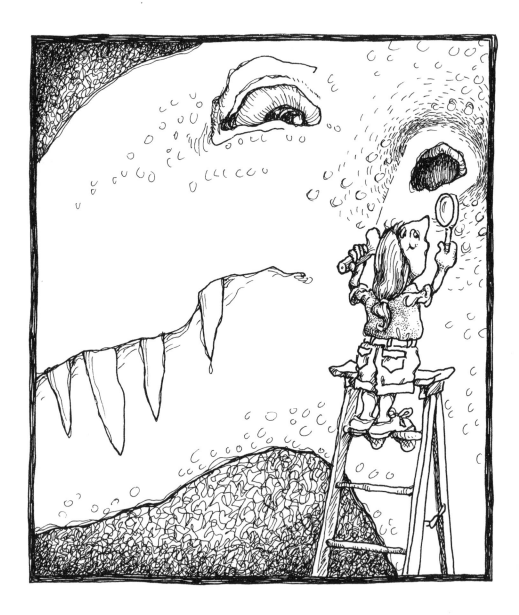

Tyrannosaurus wax.

What should you do if you dream you are in
a cave filled with iguanodons?

Wake up.

Why didn't Stegosaurus stand up straight?

He didn't want to drop the plates off his back.

What happened to the caveman who
swallowed a wheel?

It turned his stomach.

What did cave children have to eat before
they got dessert?

Their broccoli-saurus.

Why didn't Ankylosaurus dance ballet?

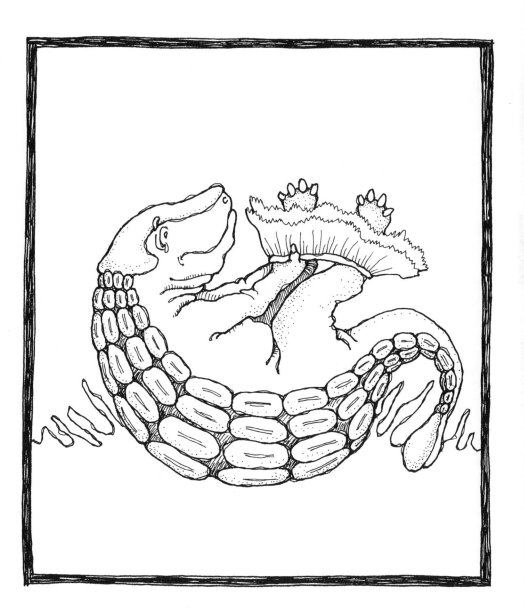

She couldn't fit into her tutu.

What did the cavemen and women say when they discovered fire?

"Now we're cooking."

How much did it cost Brachiosaurus to get
a haircut?

Ten dollars for the haircut. One dollar for the
tip. And five hundred dollars for the chair.

How did iguanodons catch flies?

With baseball gloves.

Why did so few dinosaurs fly?

Most couldn't fit in the cockpit.

Which was the fastest dinosaur?

The pronto-saurus.

Why did Brachiosaurus have such a long neck?

Because his head was so far from the rest of him.

What do dinosaurs eat for lunch?

Cream of caveman soup.

How did cavemen and women discover the sun?

It just dawned on them.

Why was the dinosaur trolly late?

It fell off its trachodon.